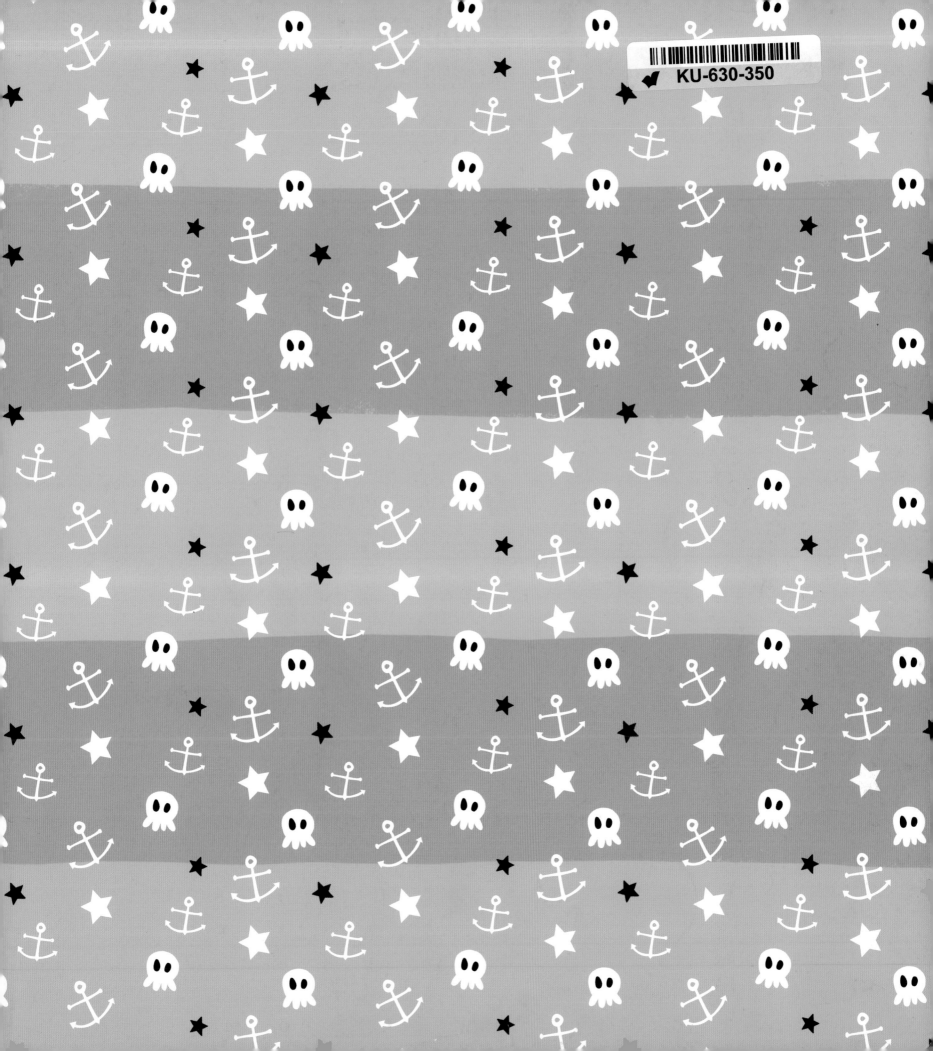

This book be for

Luca, Emilio, Lewis, Shaun, Lily, Mum, Dad

and all me shipmates!

And for you!

CATERPILLAR BOOKS
1 The Coda Centre,
189 Munster Road, London SW6 6AW
First published in Great Britain 2013
Text and illustrations copyright © Maxine Lee 2013
All rights reserved
ISBN 978-1-84857-367-3
Printed in China
CPB/1800/0255/031
1 2 3 4 5 6 7 8 9 10

This treasure belongs to:

_____

_____

A Pirates' life for us!

There be no rules on my mighty ship!

...the dark doesn't scare us!

Farewell me hearties!

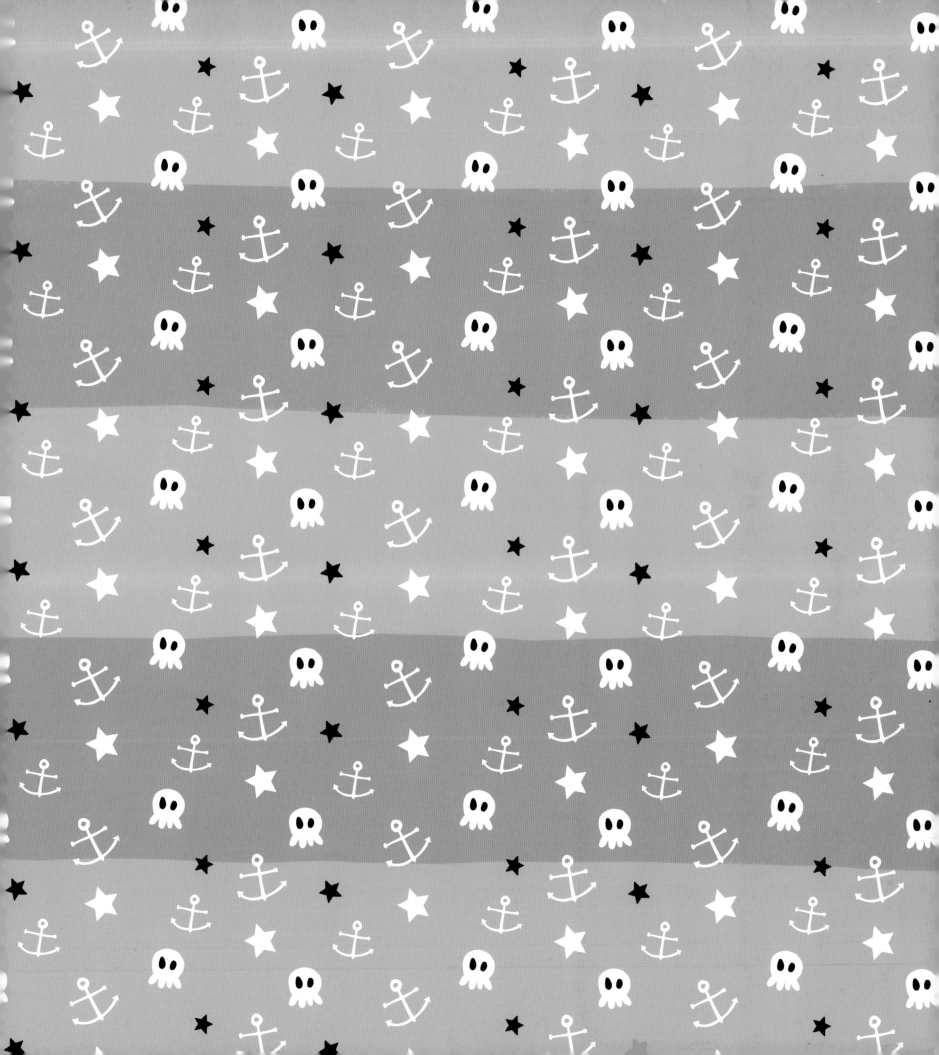

The End